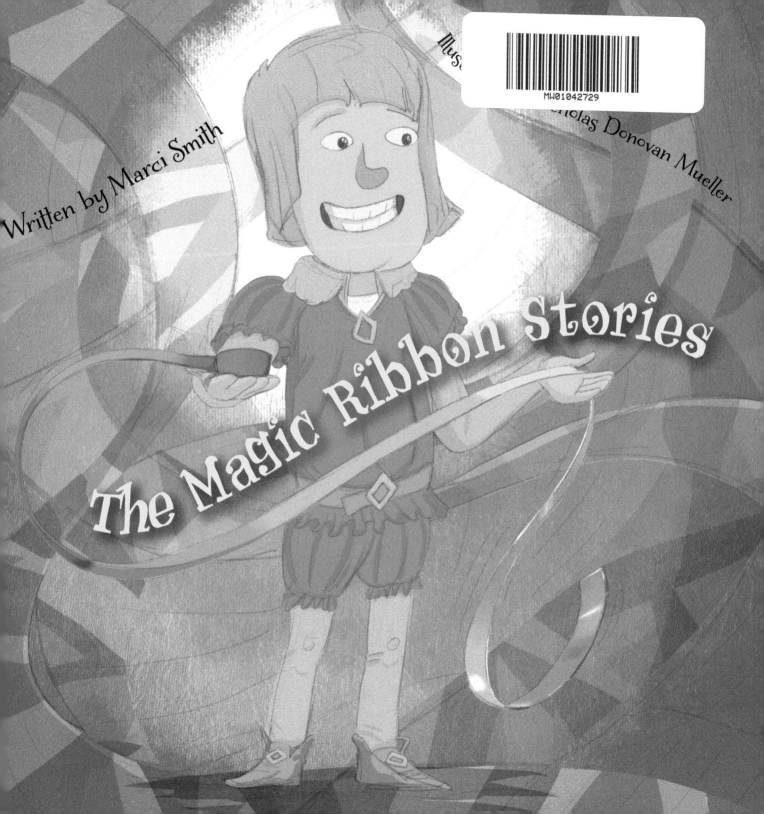

Written by Marci Smith

Illustrated by Nicholas Donovan Mueller

The Magic Ribbon Stories

Finding Flowers

Once upon a time there was a prince, named Edward, whose family ruled a land far away. Prince Edward was a very likeable person. He loved to visit the people in his kingdom, and to help them if he could. Again and again, he would be late for supper because he was chatting with a new friend, or helping an old lady with her chores. This was a problem, because supper at the castle happened on time, whether or not he was there. Prince Edward was forever eating cold food, but he never minded.

One day, his mother the Queen was getting ready for a very important dinner party. She was flying around the castle in a great state, overseeing all the arrangements, when she noticed that there were no flowers on the tables. She went to find the royal florist, only to learn he was on holiday. No one had realized – and no one had filled in!

Well! Such confusion! No flowers!

Prince Edward heard all the noise and hurried to the castle's dining room. The Queen cried, "Oh, dear, Edward! Please go out into the woods and find as many flowers as you can for the tables. We will have the loveliest table centrepieces, even with just wildflowers in the vases."

"Of course, Mother," Prince Edward agreed, and he hurried off to do his best.

Into the woods he ran, looking for flowers in all of his favourite places. But he couldn't find any! There were none where there had been many the day before. The frost overnight had wilted them all.

He walked and walked for a very long time, until he came to part of the forest that was strange to him. It was very quiet, cool, and beautiful, but he saw no flowers for the centerpieces.

The young prince felt very disappointed and sat down at the base of a tree to rest. He fell sound asleep. He dreamed of searching for flowers. In his dream, he saw large, lovely patches of wildflowers everywhere around him.

When he woke up, he looked around himself in confusion. The field around him looked completely different than it had while he dreamt! Here and there, small patches of flowers grew through the grass. They were all colours, and as pretty as Edward had ever seen but they were just too small for centerpieces.

Just a little distance away, a gurgling stream flowed busily around a tiny island. On the island were flowers of such loveliness that the Prince just *knew* he had to take them home to his mother.

Edward wandered about for a bit, admiring all the blossoms he could see from the shore. The little island was just like a jewel box, so full of gem-like flowers and plants of all sorts. Then he sat down on the bank of the stream to think about his problem. He knew he couldn't swim over to the island and swim back with his arms full of flowers. The blossoms would be destroyed by the fast-moving water.

He was very discouraged. He really didn't have time to go back to the castle for help, as the time for the party was drawing near. What would he do?

After a couple of minutes, a little humming sound caught Edward's attention. He noticed a small silver strip in the grass beside him.

When he picked it up, he saw that it was a ribbon of many colours. The end he had seen first was silver, indeed, but then it was gold and yellow and green and blue and red and orange, and purple and pink and mauve and other pretty colours. The ribbon was humming and quivering in his hand.

Edward, to his surprise, found himself talking to the ribbon. "I told my mother I would pick her flowers, and the ones on the island are just perfect. But how would I ever get them back to the castle?"

At his words the ribbon grew very still and quiet. Startled, the Prince dropped it in the grass. As he watched in amazement, the ribbon became a straight stick, very long and strong. Long enough to extend over the stream to the island without getting wet!

As if that were not strange enough, it then grew wide enough for a person to walk on. The ribbon had turned itself into a bridge for the prince!

Edward crossed the bridge carefully. After staring in wonder at the many unusual flowers for a couple of minutes, the young prince realized that he had better hurry. He scampered about, choosing flowers and plants to take back to the castle. With his arms full of sweet-smelling blossoms, he stepped carefully back onto the bridge, and in a few steps, he was off the island.

As soon as he was on the mainland again, the bridge became very narrow. It shrunk back down, and ended up at the prince's feet, a beautiful little ribbon with a silver end.

As Edward watched, the ribbon rolled into a small, neat coil, and it began to quiver and hum again.

He picked it up and spoke to the ribbon, very gently. "Thank you so much for helping me with my task, little ribbon."

It quivered and hummed some more!

Well, by now the Prince was sure the ribbon was something very special, and he knew he could not leave it behind! He carefully put down some of his flowers and put the ribbon in the pocket of his cape. Then he picked up the flowers again and made his way back to the castle.

When Prince Edward walked in with his arms full of flowers, the Queen was certainly glad to see him. She was amazed at the varieties of blooms in his arms. They quickly arranged the flowers on the tables, where they made beautiful, unusual, and colourful centerpieces.

During dinner the guests all talked about the fabulous flower displays that their hosts had created. A few asked where the flowers came from, but Prince Edward just smiled.

The Queen's dinner party was the best one ever held at the castle, and the guests all said that they were looking forward to the Queen's next invitation.

After all the guests had gone, the Queen asked, "Edward, where *did* you find such beautiful flowers?"

Prince Edward told her the whole story. She listened very carefully, and so did the King. When Edward was finished, the Queen said, "Do you know that my mother had a magic ribbon when she was a little girl? She lost it one day. Many people searched, but it was never found. I believe *you* found my mother's magic ribbon!"

The King smiled and agreed. Then he said, with a very serious look, "The magic ribbon has great power, and it can work wonders! But you must look after it and keep it with you. The magic ribbon will only work for *you*, since you are the person who found it."

A Lobster Story

One day, Prince Edward went walking through the little village that nestled at the foot of Castle Hill. He often rambled around the countryside to visit people. On this particular day, he decided to see how his friends the fishers were.

When he came to the harbour, everything was quiet. There were no singing men hauling on lines. No women yelling and selling the catch of the day. Everything was quiet. Too quiet. Prince Edward found the fishers sitting on the wharf beside their boats, mending their traps. He sat beside them and listened carefully to their stories.

They were lobster fishers, and they had been having very bad luck. The lobster traps were being broken by something, and the buoys that marked the lines were floating away. They were not finding *any* lobsters in the broken lobster traps.

They were getting very discouraged—and hungry as well! No lobster meant no pay, and no pay meant no food for their families. Things were bad indeed.

The fishers were very determined and had tried everything. First, they made the traps extra strong. Then, they bought extra strong rope to secure the buoys. Nothing seemed to work. They could not figure out what was causing all the damage!

The weather had been fine, so even though bad storms could damage the traps and lines, that was not the answer this time. Something mysterious was doing a lot of damage deep in the water!

Prince Edward thought very hard, but he couldn't help very much. The oldest of the fishers, Salty Joe, was a very good friend of the Prince and the best of the lobster fishers. He was about to go out in his boat since the tide was just right.

"May I come along?" Edward asked him quietly.

Salty Joe answered, "But of course you may come. Maybe you'll bring us luck!"

It was a lovely day, a perfect day, but no one seemed to notice. They were too sad and worried. The boats headed for the fishing area and were soon pulling up the traps that had been set out earlier. Almost every last one was broken, and there were no lobsters to be seen.

Soon the boat came to the buoy marking the biggest, strongest, newest lobster pot. The fishers had made it the day before. It had been tied with the stoutest rope they could find.

Salty Joe gave orders for it to be pulled up, and they tried. But it wouldn't come! Had they caught something too big for the trap? How would they ever find out if it wouldn't come up to the surface? Such a problem! What would they do?

Prince Edward was trying to stay out of everyone's way when, suddenly, he felt a tickle. It had come from the pocket of his cape. He put his hand into the pocket and pulled out the little silver ribbon. He had forgotten about the ribbon!

The ribbon quivered and hummed in his hand. It clearly wanted to tell him something, but what? "Little ribbon," he said, "you are quivering and humming so hard, do you want to help?"

More quivers and more hums!

Prince Edward moved closer to the side of the boat, where two fishermen were still trying to pull up the giant lobster trap with no success. He held his hand open, with the shining coil of ribbon on his palm, and watched it unroll. It showed its lovely colours: silver, and gold and yellow and green and blue and red and orange, and purple and pink and mauve and other pretty colours, too.

The startled fishers stepped back as the ribbon grow longer and longer and turned to steel. The length of steel then broke into the links of a chain, a very strong chain.

By this time everyone standing on the decks of the other boats were rubbing their eyes. They couldn't believe it! Prince Edward was holding tightly to one end of the new chain. The free end of the chain slid over the side of the boat and into the water. It followed the line of the rope leading to the new lobster pot.

After a minute in which the only thing to be heard was the rattle of the chain and the crying of the seagulls overhead, the chain pulled Prince Edward's hand! One tug. Two tugs. Three tugs!!

Edward said, "I think we should all hold the chain and pull now."

Everyone on the boat grabbed hold and pulled as hard as they could.

Nothing happened.

Salty Joe called for help from the other boats, and men and women climbed on board to join in the pulling. It worked! They began to feel something heavy coming up through the water. They began to worry. People started to shiver, afraid. Their hands grew sweaty. What could be on the end of the chain? Was it dangerous?

Finally, the trap appeared, and caught in it was one claw of a very large, very tired lobster. The lobster was so huge that it couldn't even be hauled into Salty Joe's boat! Lobster boats are not very big, you know.

The giant lobster was all bound up in the magic chain. It took four boats to haul it and the enormous trap into the harbor.

The villagers were amazed at what they saw. This lobster must have been what was destroying their traps!

When the story was told and the excitement died down, the village prepared to have a party and celebrate not having to fix their lobster traps again. There was enough lobster for the whole village, and some would be left over!

After the feast, Salty Joe made a little speech to the Prince, to say, "Thank you" on behalf of all the village.

Then he turned quietly to the Prince, who now held the little silver coil of ribbon in his hand. With a twinkle in his eye, Salty said, "From now on, when we speak of your amazing little ribbon, we will call it 'Prince Edward's Magic Lobster Ribbon.'"

Edward, smiling, put the little magic ribbon away in his pocket. Then he waved to the villagers and strolled back to the castle, whistling happily.

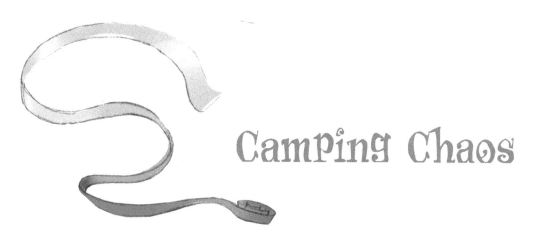

Camping Chaos

Visiting the campground which lay not far from the castle was one of good Prince Edward's favourite pastimes. He loved to meet the people who came there from all over the country, and to play with the children. He was usually there at least once a week, and he always came home with an interesting tale to tell.

One evening, however, Prince Edward became the subject of a story that was told and retold many times after.

He arrived at the campground as it was getting dark, and the usual large bonfire was being lit. It was time for toasting marshmallows and singing old songs, but something was wrong.

The children were almost all crying!

"What is the matter?" Prince Edward asked, puzzled and alarmed.

The children were crying so hard and making such a noise that they neither heard the Prince, nor could anyone else hear him. Well, obviously, something had to be done!

Prince Edward finally bellowed at one of the fathers whose children didn't seem as upset as the others, "What's the matter?"

The man looked at Prince Edward, perplexed, and beckoned him to follow him way from the noise. When they were well away from the clearing, the fire, and the children, the man said, "It's a very long sad story! You know that we are not supposed to cut branches or firewood from this area, and so we went a very long way into a part of the forest where it is allowed, and we cut some sticks that were just perfect for roasting marshmallows."

Prince Edward broke in, "That's good, I'm glad you found some. I was hoping to have roasted marshmallows tonight, too. I didn't have any dessert after supper."

"Oh, but you don't understand," the man said, "We had just arranged everything nicely on the table for the party when a big black wagon came along, pulled by two large black horses. Three men jumped out, took all the perfect marshmallow sticks, and raced off in a cloud of dust."

The Prince scowled. What awful people would steal from children? They must have had marshmallows of their own to roast.

The man continued, "Now the children are disappointed, and all the parents are angry because of the wasted afternoon."

"That certainly was a mean thing to do," the Prince said. "What shall we do about replacing those perfect sticks? Did anyone get a good look at the thieves?"

"No, the adults were busy, and the children were startled. And other than being black, the wagon looked very ordinary."

"Well," the Prince said, "let's think hard about a solution to the problem! And let's tell the children we're working on it, so they stop crying."

Prince Edward paced back and forth, trying to think of where they might find some marshmallow sticks. He scratched his head, waved away the mosquitoes that were hovering around, and paced some more. He said, "Oh, dear," about a dozen times, and then he jammed his hands into the pockets of his cape.

Immediately he felt a quiver and a hum and remembered the magic coil of silver ribbon. It was lively, as if it wanted to tell him something important. He slowly pulled it from his pocket and looked at it. It quivered and hummed even more!

"Hello, magic ribbon," he said. "I forgot you were in my pocket. What can I do for you?"

The ribbon hummed harder as if to say, "No, you've got that all wrong. I can help you!" It jumped a little and showed that Edward should carry it in the direction of the large picnic table nearby.

Oh, you want to know how it told the Prince in which direction it wanted to go? I think if you think about it hard enough, you will understand how it happened.

Down on the table, very gently, went the quivering silver coil of ribbon. The Prince stepped back to see what would happen this time. He realized that the magic ribbon had heard the whole story of the missing marshmallow sticks, but he still had no idea what the solution would be.

By this time all the children had gathered around, and the adults too, to watch the ribbon on the table.

First it unrolled, and the people gasped to see its beautiful colours. It was first silver, then gold and yellow and green and blue and red and orange, and purple and pink and mauve and every colour anyone could think of.

While they watched, the ribbon grew stiff and thick. Then it grew longer and longer and longer, until it extended way over the edges of the picnic table on both ends.

Such excitement! The children's eyes were as round as the moon that was showing over the mountaintop behind the castle. The adults were just as amazed, but they were trying to look as if this sort of thing happened every day. The children were not fooled, though, because the adults couldn't explain what was going on!

Suddenly the magic ribbon broke into many sticks, and the sticks lined up very neatly on the picnic table. The children gathered closer, and you may be sure they noticed that the sticks, which were still beautifully coloured, were just the right length for toasting marshmallows. And it looked as if there was one stick for each child!

Prince Edward handed a stick to each of the children. "You may use these for your marshmallows, but you must bring them back clean as a whistle when your parents say you have had enough!"

Gleefully, the children promised to do just that. They ran off and had a wonderful time. Not one marshmallow fell off a stick into the fire. No matter how careless the children were none of the marshmallows burned, unless the child holding the stick wanted a charred one! And the children, almost all of them, shared the sticks with their parents, who also loved toasting marshmallows. The Prince was given as many of the toasted treats as he could eat.

Finally, the children began to bring the sticks back. They put the pretty tools carefully on the picnic table, end to end, as the Prince suggested. Once they were all back, the pieces joined together again into the very long, strong straight stick. The stick shrank down to fit on the table, quivered a bit, and became a soft, shimmery ribbon, with all its colours glowing gently in the firelight.

The campers, adults, and children, all sang out at once, "Thank you, beautiful magic ribbon! What a lovely thing you did for us tonight! And thank you, Prince Edward, for coming down and bringing your helper!"

The Prince smiled happily and watched the ribbon roll itself up again with its silvery end on the outside. He picked it up, murmured, "Thank you," to the magic ribbon, and put it carefully in his pocket. He sang several songs with the campers and then trudged contentedly up the hill to the castle in the moonlight.

A Silly Fishing Adventure

One of the nicest things about the neighbourhood which lay at the bottom of Castle Hill, just past the small village, was its large saltwater swimming pool. Very often it was too cold to swim in the ocean. Other times people wanted to swim when the tide was out, but at low tide the beach was very, very wide, and very, very muddy, and swimming there was no fun at all. That's when everyone went to swim in the pool.

Carrying his towel, and his big blue cape in case it got cool, the Prince headed for the pool. It was a warm day, and the pool seemed just the answer to the sticky heat. Prince Edward's mother and father were going to come down later, to cool off in the water as well, but for now Edward was on his own.

Coming around the bend in the road on the way to the pool, Prince Edward could see people rushing here and there, looking hot and upset. *"It's too hot to rush,"* he thought. *"What are they doing?"*

As he drew closer to the pool, he saw that there was no one in it—and very, very little water, either.

All the swimmers were unhappy, and the pool woman, who was, of course, responsible for looking after the pool, was *very upset* and angry indeed.

She was shouting at her helpers and trying to write a note at the same time. There was a lot of equipment lying on the pool deck, and several people were going down a ladder into the pool with other tools. Many people were standing around and watching the confusion.

Through it all the water level was going down, down, down, slowly but surely.

When the pool woman saw Prince Edward, she put down her quill pen and rushed over, full of apologies and explanations.

"Oh, Prince Edward," she gasped, "the most awful thing is happening, and I can't seem to solve the problem, that is to say, I don't know what the problem *is*, we have been trying for hours to fix it, and it is such a hot day, and everyone is too warm and sticky and cross!"

"Hold on, there! Slow down and take it easy. I'm sure we'll find the solution soon. I guess everyone really does need to swim, especially you!" Prince Edward said with a laugh.

Prince Edward went down the ladder into the pool with the other workers. They welcomed his help, as they knew he was good at fixing things.

At first, the problem seemed simple enough. The pool worked simply: one pipe brought fresh water into the pool from the ocean, and another pipe emptied old water back into the ocean. No new water was coming into the pool, so the water level was falling.

But what was blocking the pipe? They couldn't figure it out!

The Prince and the workers tried several things to clear out the pipe, but none of them worked. Finally, the Prince climbed out and dried his face with his towel. He sat down and thought, and thought, and thought.

Soon, he noticed a funny sound. Prince Edward saw his cape, hanging on a peg outside the change house where he had left it. The sound was coming from his cape!

A funny look crossed his face, and he began to rummage in the pockets of his cape. Soon he held the quivering, humming object in his hand. Of course! It was the magic ribbon.

Edward had forgotten that it was there. He murmured, "Well, little ribbon, are you going to help us out of this pickle, too?"

The ribbon, which was so pretty, just quivered and hummed some more.

The magic ribbon seemed to want to go to the pool, so that is exactly where he took it. As the Prince stood on the bottom of the pool, the ribbon grew very long, very straight, and very stiff. Then a hook appeared on the end and the ribbon flew into the water, the Prince holding the silvery end. He held on very tightly because he had no idea what was about to happen.

More and more the ribbon pulled, and more and more of the ribbon disappeared into the blocked pipe. Soon it stopped its motion. The Prince felt three little tugs from the ribbon. Edward tried to pull the ribbon out, but he couldn't move it.

He asked for some help, and the workers came quickly over to add their weight to the job. They had been standing very still, watching the ribbon and wondering what was going to happen next. They were a little afraid, although they had heard some strange stories of the magic ribbon helping out in other places.

Of course, the swimmers from far away places hadn't heard any of the tales, so they were very concerned, indeed. They held onto their children, kept them quiet, and watched very carefully.

It seemed a very long time that Prince Edward and his helpers had to pull the ribbon, and there were yards and yards of ribbon coiled at their feet. Then they pulled one last time, and something came loose on the other end of the ribbon. The workers all fell backwards in a heap, with Prince Edward on top.

When they picked themselves up and looked down into the pool, they saw that there was water flowing into the pool again. And they saw a very big Silly Fish attached to the hook on the other end of the magic ribbon.

Now, I don't know if you are familiar with Silly Fish, but they are just what the name implies: silly fish. They get into all sorts of mischief because they hardly ever think about what they are about to do. If they do think, they seem to think upside down so that everything they try turns out wrong. The Silly Fish are a great nuisance, especially on hot summer days!

This particular fish was looking very foolish indeed. When the men pulled the fish out of the water, he said, "Oh, my! I am so glad you got me out of that place. I only wanted to see where that pipe went, and no one would tell me, so I had to swim in and find out for myself! And then I got stuck. Oh, my! Isn't this a nice pool—but it doesn't have enough water in it. Why don't you fill it up some more?"

The pool woman choked on an angry reply, and Prince Edward growled, "Silly Fish, you ought to be put in an aquarium! You are the reason that there is not enough water in this pool. You blocked the pipe! We expect an apology!"

The Silly Fish looked very unhappy and said slowly, "But, I didn't mean any harm. Oh, my! This is the third bit of trouble I've been in this week. I am so sorry!"

The pool woman spoke up., "What shall we do with this little monster, Prince Edward?"

Prince Edward replied, "I think we might dump him in that pond with the goldfish. Won't that be a good punishment for him? They will tickle him terribly at every opportunity."

"Oh, please, not that!" gulped the Silly Fish. "If you will put me back into the bay, I will go away and never bother you again, I promise."

"Very well, then. But remember, if we find you here again, it's into the goldfish pond with you!"

The pool woman nodded her agreement, and with Edward's help she scooped the Silly Fish into a large pail.

"Here," she said to one of her helpers, "take this nuisance to the bay and let's get on with clearing away all this equipment. And let's have a good look at the special tool the Prince found to help us."

Everyone turned to the Prince and looked at the ribbon which dangled from his hand. Embarrassed at the attention it was getting, the magic ribbon shrunk back to its normal size. The hook on the end straightened out, the stiffness disappeared, and all the beautiful colours sparkled in the sun.

The ribbon shook a bit to scatter the drops of water from its sides, then it coiled itself up again, with the silvery end on the outside, just as it always was.

It lay on the palm of Prince Edward's hand and listened to the wonderful words of praise from everyone standing around. Prince Edward put the magic ribbon in the pool woman's office, thinking that he had better remember to take it home that afternoon.

Just before the King and Queen came down the hill for a swim, the pool woman announced that there was now enough water in the pool, and that it was safe for swimming again.

There was a good deal of chatter around the pool that afternoon, as everyone who came to swim wanted to know the whole story. And when they heard the story, some of the people just couldn't believe it.

But you believe it, don't you?

The people, who felt much cooler and happier after their swim, all said that they would certainly come back to that community again because of the wonderful pool!

Tug of war

One winter day Prince Edward walked down to the village wearing the snowshoes that he had just received for Christmas. He met several villagers who stopped to chat and ask the Prince how he liked travelling on his fancy new "skis". He trampled around to show how they worked, and the people were very interested.

They all went off, talking about snowshoes. *"It would be fun to supply a few pairs to the village, so everyone could try them,"* the Prince thought. *"They must surely be made in sizes for children, too."*

In the village, something strange was happening. There was a lot of music and noise, laughter and yelling. It was the Annual Winter Festival! The Prince had forgotten all about it. As he wandered around he found a place where there was going to be a tug of war.

This was a very popular activity every year; so popular, in fact, that there were several teams waiting impatiently to try their muscles against friends, neighbours, and relatives. But something was not quite right.

The mayor of the village rushed over to the Prince. "Sir," he said, "we have a problem. The big rope for the tug of war contest is missing! It's nowhere to be found! Do you have your magic ribbon in your pocket? Maybe it could help us?"

"Gee," said the Prince, "I don't know. I got dressed in a hurry this morning and I don't remember if I put it in my pocket." He patted all his pockets, and finally felt the ribbon vibrating in one of the pockets he never used. He pulled it out. "Ha!" he exclaimed. "Here it is!"

To the Mayor he said, "How shall we work this? How much rope do you need?"

Before the Mayor could answer, the ribbon slowly unrolled itself, showing its beautiful colours: silver, and gold and yellow and green and blue and red and orange, and purple and pink and mauve and other pretty colours, too.

The ribbon became a rope perfect for tug of war. Edward gave both ends to the Mayor, who gave one end to the leader of Team One and the other end to the leader of Team Two. Everyone could see all the wonderful colours in the rope, which was the perfect length and thickness for tug of war.

The mayor blew the whistle to start the contest. Everything was going along as usual with tug of war and then the magic ribbon started to make the game more interesting. Soon people watching started to laugh. The magic ribbon was very active in the contest, pulling first this way then that way, up and down, so the team members were laughing and wobbling and falling in a heap.

They were pulled left and right and very quickly and strongly, so there were several people being dumped in the snow or pulled around in silly circles. They were all hooting with laughter and trying to stand up, but they couldn't do so! The people watching the contest were very amused and shouting out directions, but nothing and nobody was being helpful. Nothing was strong enough!

When the Mayor blew the whistle for the game to stop and for the next teams to pull, teams Three and Four took over.

The leader of Team Four said to everyone, "Just watch, we will show you how to do this!"

Team Three was howling with laughter at this silly boast but feeling strong and capable. They knew it was unlikely that they could control the rope, but they vowed to try their hardest. They were shoved and pulled around. They wobbled and fell just as Team One and Two had, been but a little more quickly.

The onlookers were having such fun watching Team Three and Team Four, and hoping they themselves would not be challenged to play this crazy game any time soon.

They all said, "It's fun to watch!" and, "We'll try next year!"

When the Mayor blew the whistle to stop the game and the pulling stopped, all the pullers were covered in snow, hatless, breathless, tired, and happy that they had so much fun in such an unusual way!

They watched in amazement as the rope shook off the remaining snow and became a magic ribbon again. It rolled itself up: first the wonderful colours and then the gold and silver parts on the outside. It was ready just

in time to hear the Mayor declare that although the four teams tried very hard, the magic ribbon/rope was the winner of both contests.

Everyone shouted a big, *"Thank you!"* to the magic ribbon. The cheers and shouts and laughter were heard everywhere around the village.

There was also a big, *"Thank you!"* to the Prince, who was shaking his head in wonder, hardly believing what had happened in the village that day

Soon the magic ribbon was safely back in Edward's pocket. Hot chocolate and cookies were served.

The Mayor spoke quietly to the Prince and said, "I hope we never find that dirty old rope! We had such fun with this one, and it is so beautiful too. Thank you for sharing it with us."

The Prince strolled home still shaking his head and wondering what the magic ribbon would do next.

About the Author

I hope you enjoy these little tales - I enjoyed making them up. Marci Smith. It was so easy!

Marci Smith is a mother of two and Gemma to five grandchildren. She was born in Edmonton, Alberta lived her youth in Beauharnois, Quebec, and spent her early married life in Montreal, Quebec and London, Ontario. She has called Barrie, Ontario home for many years. Marci was an Administrative Assistant, Lifeguard and Swimming Instructor before retiring and she continues to read, craft and create.

In the 1970s, Marci's family took camping trips from Barrie to the Canadian east and west coasts and these stories were initially the product of those trips due to missing story books.

As the stories were shared at sleepovers and family gatherings, Marci's nieces and nephews often asked that these stories be written down. At long last, here they are! Auntie Marci is sorry that you had to wait such a long time!

"There is no strain involved in writing *The Magic Ribbon Stories*. Little problems just seemed to arrive without any fuss and every challenge was solved immediately by the Magic Ribbon, making many adults giggle with me."

FriesenPress

One Printers Way
Altona, MB R0G 0B0
Canada

www.friesenpress.com

Illustrated by Nicholas Donovan Mueller

ISBN
978-1-03-830697-5 (Hardcover)
978-1-03-830696-8 (Paperback)
978-1-03-830698-2 (eBook)

1. JUVENILE FICTION, FANTASY & MAGIC

Distributed to the trade by The Ingram Book Company

www.ingramcontent.com/pod-product-compliance
Lightning Source LLC
Jackson TN
JSHW071442270125
77796JS00006B/24